MIGHTY MAX
AND THE LOST C

by Terry Kinnear

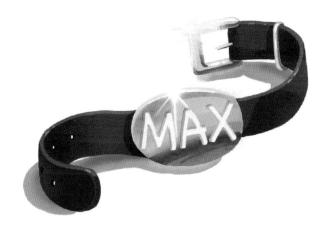

Illustrated by Stephen Millingen

In a picturesque village,
  beside railway tracks,

Lived a boy they called Jack
  and his kitten named Max.

One day after school
Jack came home quite upset,

And was greeted with "purrr"
from his sweet, loving pet.

"There's a hole in my schoolbag
and just as I feared,

A few things are missing;
they've just disappeared!"

"My sport socks
for gym class,

my paint set
and glue

and a shiny new collar
I made
just for you!"

"A shiny new collar
Jack made
just for me,

I've just got to have it, but where could it be?"

Determined to find it,
Max sprang to his feet,

He leapt through the catflap
and dashed down the street.

He was prowling along,
    when he came to the well,

Where he picked up a scent,
    "eww, what is that smell?"

"Could that be my collar,

behind those big rocks?"

"**NO**... it's a dog
with some smelly old socks!"

"Scat little cat!
It's not safe to be out,
haven't you heard who's been roaming about?"

"The biggest and meanest of dogs on this street,
A kitten like you he would eat as a treat!"

"Well I'm not afraid,
he's not met me before,

Cause I'm Mighty Max,
you just wait till I roar!"

So Max carried on
up and over the brook.

He heard a big 'squelch'
and he went down to look.

"Is my collar down here,

Where the water runs through?"

"Teehee," giggled Max.
"It's the paint set and glue!"

"Hey split, little kit!
You need to turn back,
Haven't you heard
who's been seen near the track?"

"The hungriest dog, so much bigger than you!
He'll swallow you whole and he won't need to
chew!"

"Well I'm not afraid, he's not met me before,
Cause I'm Mighty Max,
you just wait till I roar!"

He didn't turn tail
    he just kept on instead,

Then spotted a twinkle
    not too far ahead.

"Could that be my collar
    right there by the gate?

YES - but OH-NO..."

"... I'm afraid I'm too late!"
The dog had it clenched
in its bloodthirsty jaws,

He walked straight toward Max
with his razor-sharp claws.

The giant dog snarled, "What a sweet, tasty snack!"

"That's my collar." cried Max. "Now you must give it back!"

"You think you can take back
this collar from me?

Before you can blink, I'll have
kitten for tea!"

"You should be scared,
    you've not met me before,

Cause I'm Mighty Max,
    you just wait till I roar!"

Then brave little Max opened up his small jaw
and stretched out his neck to let out a huge

roar!

When just from behind
on the old railway tracks...

...The loudest of roars thundered up behind Max,
As just then a railway train slammed on its brake,

and echoed a roar
that made everything

"T-t-take it!"

he spluttered, then scuttled away,

He had messed with
the wrong little kitten that day.

For Max was the mightiest kitten in town,

One brave little kitten who never backs down.

13460303R00016

Printed in Great Britain
by Amazon.co.uk, Ltd.,
Marston Gate.